Eva's Heart

inspired by
true events

Sue Milo
illustrations by Samantha Brown

Balboa Press books may be ordered through booksellers or by contacting:

Balboa Press
A Division of Hay House
1663 Liberty Drive
Bloomington, IN 47403
www.balboapress.com
1 (877) 407-4847

ISBN: 978-1-5043-6392-1 (sc)
ISBN: 978-1-5043-6393-8 (e)

Library of Congress Control Number: 2016912975

Print information available on the last page.

Balboa Press rev. date: 10/24/2016

This book belongs to

Alyssa Baycі

This beloved book is dedicated to Wendy and her two delightful daughters, Ryan and Jaden. Their consistent love, compassion, and devotion for my furry family eternally warms my heart.

In addition, I would like to include my young friend Niki in this dedication. She will always be a special star in my universe.

Eva's Heart

inspired by
true events

Hi! My name is Eva and boy, do I have a story for you!

It all started when I was born. (I was the cutest puppy, if I do say so myself!) My family at the time did not have enough money to raise me. They were wonderful, though, so they took me to live at a beautiful shelter where I would be safe and loved.

They absolutely adored me at the shelter.
They gave me training so I could impress
my new family someday.
I never got sad because I
knew in my HEART
She was coming
for me. I just
KNEW it!

One day, a nice couple adopted me. They really liked me and I was a very good girl, but something didn't FEEL right....because it wasn't HER. Their lives were very busy and they didn't have enough time for me, so they returned me to the shelter. But, I wasn't sad because I knew in my HEART....She was coming for me.

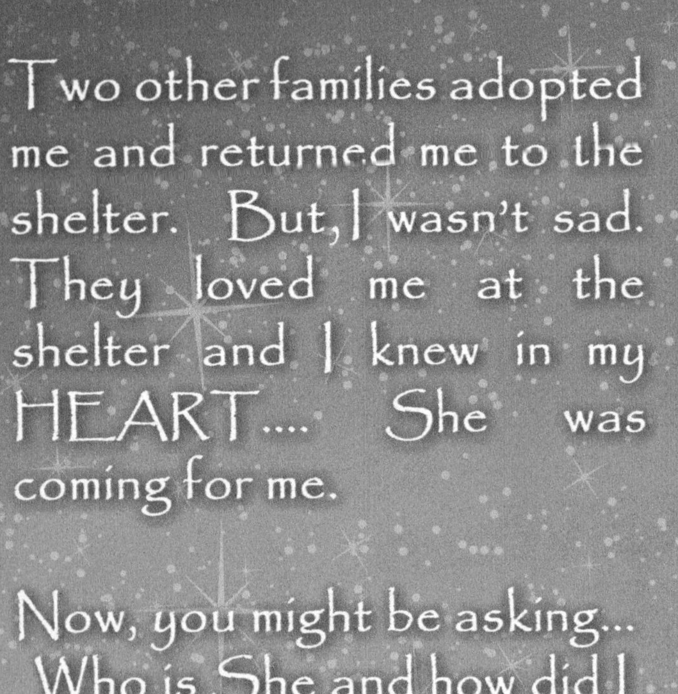

Two other families adopted me and returned me to the shelter. But, I wasn't sad. They loved me at the shelter and I knew in my HEART.... She was coming for me.

Now, you might be asking... Who is She and how did I know She was coming for me? Good questions!

ANIMAL
SHELTER

"She" is my Forever Mom who is going to love me with all her heart forever. I KNEW she was coming because .... now this is the magical part .... because an angel called Bonjo visited and told me!

Angel Bonjo was so cute and so funny. I loved him instantly! He said that only I could see and hear him, but he was there to help with a miracle. He told me the most wonderful stories of his life with his Forever Mom and his sister before he went to heaven. Bonjo and his sister Chloe went on vacations with her. They went swimming, boating, running and playing. His mom took them on long walks through the forest and they had such FUN!

Bonjo's mom was very sad without him. His sister, Chloe, was very sad, too. His mom and Chloe were trying to cheer each other up, but Chloe was old now, too, and she wasn't feeling very well.

Angel Bonjo told me I would be PERFECT for his mom. Can you believe it? Me, EVA! I was so excited, sometimes I couldn't calm down. He said, "Eva, you must be patient, because she will come for you. I will help."

HELP? How was Angel Bonjo going to help? But, he told me to never lose hope. It would happen if I believed it in my HEART.

On a rainy, cold Saturday afternoon in February, Angel Bonjo's mom and Chloe were taking a nap and the craziest thing happened! Angel Bonjo's mom had a dream that she would have a puppy named EVA! It was so real, she told one of her friends that she didn't think it was a dream. Angel Bonjo was laughing in heaven because, of course, he helped his mom dream of me, EVA!

A week later, his mom was sad about a lot of things and she decided to stop in at a grand opening of a new pet store. She knew they had adoption events on weekends and sometimes she would go to cheer up. She didn't think she wanted another dog right now because she missed Bonjo so much, but she went in anyway to have a smile. She just wanted to play with the puppies.

Guess who was at the adoption event at that store on that Saturday? Me, EVA of course! Now, Angel Bonjo told me to be extra well behaved and look beautiful (I always do!) as today might be the day I met my Forever Mom.

Here is the BIG moment....My Forever Mom came around the corner aisle in the store and there I was. (I knew it was HER the minute I saw her.) I had a jacket on that said 'I am selling kisses for $1'." She immediately smiled and took out some money and put it in my jacket. She was so impressed with me because I was behaving so beautifully. She was kneeling and petting me for a long time.

Kisses
$1

A volunteer named Wendy was holding my leash and was talking to her. When she stood up to leave, Angel Bonjo said to me, "Quick, Eva, sit on your back legs like this...Quick, Quick, Quick, before she leaves!"

I did the trick so fast I was afraid I would fall over! (I had never done it before!) She stopped and looked at me, so shocked. This was a special trick Angel Bonjo used to do for her when he wanted to make her laugh.

And then, here's the greatest part. Wendy, the volunteer, said, "Oh look, Eva really likes you!"

See, my Forever Mom didn't know my name before this moment, so she said to Wendy, "What did you say?"

Wendy said, "Eva really likes you. She is doing a new trick for you."

"Eva really likes you!"

Well, my Forever Mom's eyes filled with tears and she started to cry as she remembered her special boy, Bonjo, and as she remembered her special dream of Eva. And because she KNEW in her HEART something very loving and special had happened: a miracle!

When she told Wendy her dream, it seemed meant to be I would go home with her. She was worried, though, that Chloe might not like me because she hadn't loved any other dog except Bonjo.

But Wendy said, "Don't worry about a thing. I am a dog trainer and I will help Chloe get adjusted to little Eva." Wendy was so great and she helped Chloe and me get acquainted. When Chloe first met me, she even gave me a kiss! How about that? (I think Angel Bonjo helped out on this, too, don't you?)

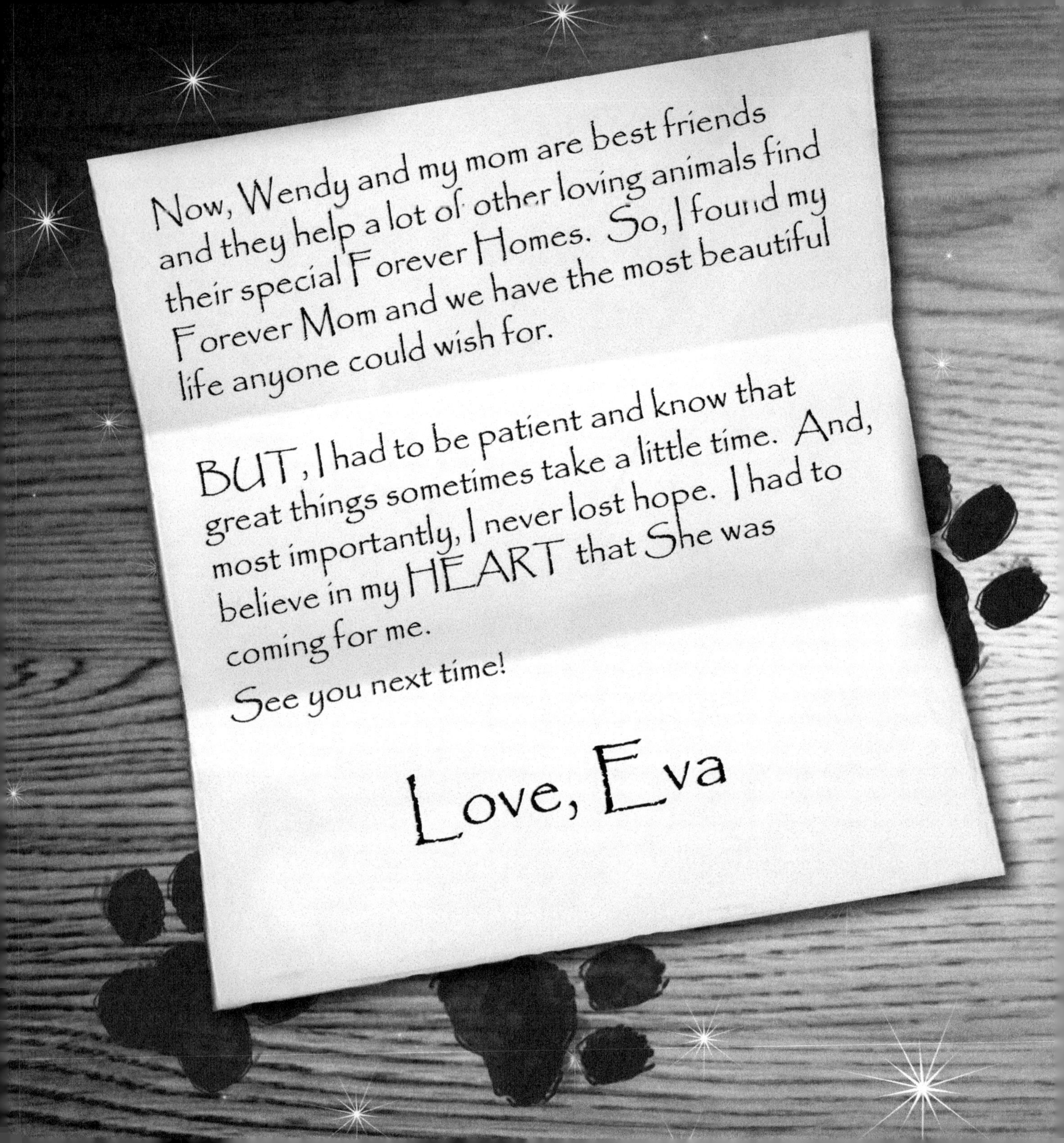

Now, Wendy and my mom are best friends and they help a lot of other loving animals find their special Forever Homes. So, I found my Forever Mom and we have the most beautiful life anyone could wish for.

BUT, I had to be patient and know that great things sometimes take a little time. And, most importantly, I never lost hope. I had to believe in my HEART that She was coming for me.

See you next time!

Love, Eva

Ah...
Thanks, Mom
I knew you'd
find me!

CPSIA information can be obtained
at www.ICGtesting.com
Printed in the USA
LVOW06s1100031216
515006LV00031BA/157/P